www.randomhouse.com/kids

Library of Congress Cataloging-in-Publication Data:
Lenski, Lois, 1893–1974
Mr. and Mrs. Noah / by Lois Lenski.
p. cm.
Summary: Mr. Noah builds an ark that holds his family and the animals
during the forty days of the flood.
ISBN 0-375-81076-5 (trade) — ISBN 0-375-91076-X (lib. bdg.)
1. Noah's ark—Juvenile fiction. [1. Noah's ark—Fiction. 2. Noah (Biblical figure)—
Fiction. 3. Animals—Fiction. 4. Deluge—Fiction.] I. Title.
PZ7.L54 Mi 2002
[E]—dc21
2001019696

First Random House Edition
Printed in the United States of America   January 2002   10 9 8 7 6 5 4 3 2 1
RANDOM HOUSE and colophon are registered trademarks of Random House, Inc.

MR. and MRS. NOAH

LOIS LENSKI

Random House  New York

Once there was a man
called Mr. Noah.
His wife was Mrs. Noah.

God told Mr. Noah
to build an Ark.
Mr. Noah brought boards
and set to work.

Noah had three sons.
Their names were
Shem,
Ham,
and Japheth.

Noah's sons helped
build the Ark.
It was like a house on a boat.
Shem sawed boards in two,
Ham hammered nails,
and Japheth painted
the roof red.

At last the Ark was done.
The sun was shining,
but God told Mr. Noah
it was going to rain.
God told Mr. Noah
to put all the animals
inside the Ark.

Mr. and Mrs. Noah
  called the tame animals,
and they all came,
  two by two.
There were dogs and cats,
  and pigs and sheep,
    and cows and horses.
They all went
  into the Ark.

Shem called the birds,
and they all came,
two by two.
There were red birds and blue birds,
and hens and roosters,
and ducks and geese,
and flamingoes and pelicans.
They all went into the Ark.

Ham called the insects,
and they all came,
two by two.
There were flies and mosquitoes,
and moths and butterflies,
and worms and grasshoppers,
and ants and spiders,
and bugs and beetles.
They all went into the Ark.

Japheth called the wild animals,
and they all came,
two by two.
There were turtles and rabbits,
and bears and camels,
and elephants and giraffes.
They all went
into the Ark.

Then it began to rain.
Mrs. Noah called
Shem, Ham, and Japheth.
"Come into the Ark," said Mrs. Noah,
"so you won't get wet."
So they came in.

It kept on raining.
It rained harder
and harder.
"We must go in," said Mrs. Noah,
"so we won't get wet."
So they went in.

It rained and rained.
The rain covered up
all the houses
and the trees.
The Ark was like a boat.
It floated on the water.

The animals lived
  inside the Ark.
It was very crowded.
Mr. and Mrs. Noah kept order.
It was raining outside.

Noah's sons helped
take care
of the animals.
Shem fed them
three times a day.
They were very hungry.

Ham helped, too.
He gave the animals
water to drink.
They were very thirsty.

Japheth helped, too.
He swept up the crumbs
from the floor
three times a day.

It kept on raining
     for forty days and forty nights.
          The sun did not shine.
The Ark rocked up and down
          on the waves.
     Everybody had to stay inside.

At last it stopped raining.
And then the sun came out!
The animals were glad
to see the sunshine.
They wanted to get out,
but there was water
all around.

Then Mr. Noah said,
"Fly away, little white dove!
Find the leaf of a tree
and bring it back to me!"
So the white dove flew away
across the waters.

Soon the white dove flew back
    with a green leaf in her bill.
        The waters went down.
The Ark came to rest
                on a hill.
    Noah opened the door of the Ark,
    and all the animals
                came out.

Mr. and Mrs. Noah
came out of the Ark.
Shem, Ham, and Japheth
came out, too.
They were glad.

Noah and his family
    gave thanks to God.
And God made a rainbow
        in the sky.
The grass grew
    and pretty flowers bloomed,
    and the world was
        beautiful.

*And
that's all
about
Mr. and Mrs. Noah!*